MINI SAGAS

THE ADVENTURE STARTS HERE 2009 ...

TALES FROM THE EAST MIDLANDS

First published in Great Britain in 2009 by
Young Writers, Remus House, Coltsfoot Drive,
Peterborough, PE2 9JX
Tel (01733) 890066 Fax (01733) 313524
All Rights Reserved

© Copyright Contributors 2009
SB ISBN 978-1-84924 254 7

FOREWORD

Young Writers was established in 1990 with the aim of encouraging and nurturing writing skills in young people and giving them the opportunity to see their work in print. By helping them to become more confident and expand their creative skills, we hope our young writers will be encouraged to keep writing as they grow.

Secondary school pupils nationwide have been exercising their minds to create their very own short stories, using no more than fifty words, to be included here in our latest competition *The Adventure Starts Here 2009 ... .*

The entries we received showed an impressive level of technical skill and imagination, an absorbing look into the eager minds of our future authors.

CONTENTS

King Edward VII School, Melton Mowbray

Newbridge High School, Coalville

THE MINI SAGAS

CC IS ALONE

(Inspired by 'Chinese Cinderella' by Adeline Yen Mah)

As she saw the ants climb the rock, their courage gave CC strength. With her new-found bravery, she went to find the acrobat boys. Despair hit her like a bullet when they were no longer there, but a kind man directed her to where they would be. New hope!

JENNI LITTLEHALES (12)

Alderman White School & Language College, Bramcote

1

CHINESE CINDERELLA

(Inspired by 'Chinese Cinderella' by Adeline Yen Mah)

As CC stepped onto the street, frightened and alone, she saw the homeless and hungry staring her in the face. Was this her fate? When she got to the park, not seeing the acrobats who brought her joy, she felt gutted! Then, at a back stall, there was hope …

ISLA PALMER (12)

Alderman White School & Language College, Bramcote

UNTITLED

Black sheets covered the empty town, shadows on every corner. Wind whistled through dark alleyways between stretched buildings. Evil crept through the streets. Strange whispers closed in, twisting your mind. 'Is there anyone there?' No voice replied, just the voices you once heard. Just letting you know, you're not alone.

HOLLY STARK (14)
Alderman White School & Language College, Bramcote

WAR

Shell after shell slammed into the ground, hundreds in the first volley. Like screaming angels of death, they descended upon us. No glory exists in war and supposed heroes are always the first to die. The only release from the chaos is death.

MAX EMMETT (12)

Alderman White School & Language College, Bramcote

THE REGRETS OF CHINESE CINDERELLA

(Inspired by 'Chinese Cinderella' by Adeline Yen Mah)

I shouldn't have done that. I feel so worthless, so stupid! Why don't they understand? I'm petrified! There's nobody in the whole world who can help. I'm the most unwanted person ever! But I must carry on with my shattered pride and my reckless head. But I can't, I'm alone …

HAZEL FORD (12)

Alderman White School & Language College, Bramcote

WAITING FOR DEATH

A scream echoes around me. How can you laugh?
Flames rise quickly, why can't I breathe? Blood
runs down my face, dripping to the floor below.
I'm waiting for the darkness to come - hurry.
Flames lick at my body. Why me? Slowly, slowly
the darkness comes. The screaming ends …

FRANCES PEARSON (14)

Alderman White School & Language College, Bramcote

LOSING MY HOME

(Inspired by 'Chinese Cinderella' by Adeline Yen Mah)

Sitting in the darkness, I stared. Nowhere to go.
Nowhere to hide. There was a constant, *drip,
drip!* and scuttling of rats. As I looked around I
saw a child for sale, all tattered and torn. Now I
thought sooner or later I would be in the same
position.

FRANCESCA WOOD (12)

Alderman White School & Language College, Bramcote

7

JAPANESE CRUELTY IN WWII

(Inspired by 'Chinese Cinderella' by Adeline Yen Mah)

I couldn't breathe, heavy hobnail boots of the Japanese soldiers catapulted into my sides. I wheezed at passers-by, imploring them for help, but the suppressed fear was evident in the onlookers' eyes, denying me assistance. My abusers walked off, laughing cruelly as they went. 'Next time,' one cried, 'bow!'

PHILIPPA SMITH (12)

Alderman White School & Language College, Bramcote

OUT IN THE COLD

(Inspired by 'Chinese Cinderella' by Adeline Yen Mah)

I became homeless in just a few seconds. I was full of rage and felt rejected. All I wanted was a place to call home. Looking for a safe place to be, a sanctuary to go to. I saw slaves being beaten to the ground. I felt alone.

BEN STEVENSON (12)
Alderman White School & Language College, Bramcote

9

ALONE

(Inspired by 'Chinese Cinderella' by Adeline Yen Mah)

Bam … ! The door was slammed behind me. I felt as if all the happiness had been sucked out of the world. I staggered into the dark, frosty night, not knowing where I would end up. I felt cold … I had no home, no money and no food. I was alone.

MITCHELL POYZER (13)

Alderman White School & Language College, Bramcote

CHOICES

(Inspired by 'Chinese Cinderella' by Adeline Yen Mah)

How could she not see that woman was trouble?
She paced across the room, before sitting down
in her chair by the fire. She sighed, looking up at
the cold, black sky. Someone cast out would not
survive even a few days, but it would have to be
done ...

CONRAD DUNCAN (12)

Alderman White School & Language College, Bramcote

11

WRATH OF THE STEPMOTHER

(Inspired by 'Chinese Cinderella' by Adeline Yen Mah)

The evil was plain in her eyes. She swept across the floor pacing back and forth. Waiting, waiting, for her prey to come and cower before her, then move in for the kill. She stopped, listening, the hate rising inside. An icy smile tugged at the corners of her mouth …

LISA BARRETT (12)

Alderman White School & Language College, Bramcote

HOPELESS

(Inspired by 'Chinese Cinderella' by Adeline Yen Mah)

Was this going to be the end for poor CC? All
we could see was despair! Soon after she had
a dreadful battle with her stepmother, all she
could do was sulk. She was hopeless, helpless,
homeless. Was there any sign of hope?

PETER MCCOLL (12)

Alderman White School & Language College, Bramcote

13

THE DAY BEFORE CHRISTMAS

It was the day before Christmas. The snow was floating in the air, dropping to the ground. Children playing on their sleighs, gliding down the hills, and far away, Santa came out to play. Tears of laughter as Santa rolled in a ball. Sun comes down, can't wait for dawn.

PAIGE BROOKS (14)

Alderman White School & Language College, Bramcote

ALONE

(Inspired by 'Chinese Cinderella' by Adeline Yen Mah)

CC saw the soldiers march by. It reminded her of what happened once … She stood on the sidewalk trembling, fearing it would happen to her too. One of the soldiers shot a man. As soon as she heard the shot, fear gripped her, petrified her. She felt absolutely helpless.

MARTYN BOND (12)

Alderman White School & Language College, Bramcote

A MURDEROUS TALE

I stood there, peering out of the window, down at the pavement. I quickly spotted my target, a middle-aged man, and I ran down the stairs. As I walked out the doorway, I followed my target into an alley. I stood behind him, and quickly stabbed him. Job done!

JAMES PEARSON (14)

Alderman White School & Language College, Bramcote

CHINESE CINDERELLA (THROWN OUT)

(Inspired by 'Chinese Cinderella' by Adeline Yen Mah)

I couldn't live with myself if I had done anything like that! Rejecting his own daughter; and that stepmother was cackling behind him! Now I don't even have a big aunt to go back to! But, Dad wouldn't normally even dream about rejecting me. Grandma Wu could be an option ...

MATTHEW SMITH (12)

Alderman White School & Language College, Bramcote

17

HUNTING FOR GLORY

I aimed down the scope, pressing it into my eye because of the tension I was under. I inhaled heavily to help steady myself. The target's head was comfortably in the line of my hunting crosshairs, yet I felt something was wrong. Oh well. Five, four, three, two, one, *bang!*

BEN BLOOMFIELD (13)

Alderman White School & Language College, Bramcote

AWAY

I thought I would only be out for a few hours, if that. I thought wrong. I watched them grieve over my pale, dead body. I screamed for them to stop, then the lid covered the coffin. My face was away forever, never to be seen by my family again.

BETH BARKLEY (13)

Alderman White School & Language College, Bramcote

A GOOD NIGHT'S SLEEP

I see it in my dreams and when I close my eyes it doesn't stop. It's always there, waiting for me to close my sleepy eyes. It wants me, it needs me, but it can't ever get me. Not until I die. Not until everyone dies …

BRIDIE COPE (13)

Alderman White School & Language College, Bramcote

HER

It was my turn next. I was mostly scared of the scissors. I like my hair the way it was. It was time, they called my name. as she approached me I closed my eyes. When I opened them, my hair was on the floor. I liked my haircut.

CHARLOTTE MALTBY (13)

Alderman White School & Language College, Bramcote

WALKING STICK

There I was, walking through the forest. That's when I saw an old lady walking towards me, holding a basket and a walking stick in either hand. She suddenly disappeared, leaving her basket and walking stick behind. Where did she go without the walking stick that she left behind?

VICKI WOOD (13)

Alderman White School & Language College, Bramcote

THREE HEADED

It was dark. There it lay. Still, like it was dead. Flies were buzzing above. I think they were having a party. I looked around. It woke up, looking at me. It's a dog but then it grew and grew - one head, two heads, three heads. Run fast! Now! *Bang!*

ABIGAIL SKINNER (14)
Alderman White School & Language College, Bramcote

MY PRIZE

Creeping past the sleeping guard, who I'd
drugged earlier. I ran through the lasers which
guarded my prize. Snatching it, I ran.
You will never guess what I stole …

CASSEY BELL (13)

Alderman White School & Language College, Bramcote

THE LIGHT

'The light,' I screamed, pointing upwards. No one was there … It was as if I wasn't wanted. *'Ouch!'* I looked up, it was getting brighter. I held my hand out and looked down. I saw my family. They looked upset. I already knew. I knew I was in Heaven.

EMMA NICOLE SANDERSON (14)

Alderman White School & Language College, Bramcote

THE LIFE OF A GANGSTER

A 'G' is another word for a gangster. They walk on the street with thoughts of murder. Gangsters are the kind of people with a dream, always thinking about hip-hop. In their songs, all they talk about is hustling, pimping, guns and girls. Something must be done. *Help me!*

BENEDICTA OWUSU-AMANKWAATIA (14)

Alderman White School & Language College, Bramcote

GANGSTER BEAN

One day a normal bean was walking down the street, when he suddenly saw some beans fighting. Instead of walking away like a normal bean, he became a gangster bean, went up to them and kicked them in the bum. They all went away and never had a fight again.

BEN TAYLOR (12)

Alderman White School & Language College, Bramcote

THE DAY SANTA NEVER CAME

It was a cold, gloomy night. The lights were flickering on and off, when, 'Ho, ho, ho!' Santa appeared on the roof. A little boy tried to watch, but Santa never came down the chimney. The boy stayed there till morning. The stars twinkled, knowing he deserved it.

JACK SPRAY (11)

Alderman White School & Language College, Bramcote

PAUL O'GRADY SHOW

Welcome to the Morning Show with Paul O'Grady and Buster the dog. Suddenly ... *boom!* Toxic gas covers the studio and Girls Aloud run in and steal Buster. They escape in their pink bus! Paul O'Grady is cancelled. Everyone has a great big party after that!

SAM CROSBY (12)

Alderman White School & Language College, Bramcote

CHRISTMAS

It was a cold Christmas morning. I woke up and ran downstairs. My mum and dad handed me my presents and I ripped the wrapping paper. I opened the big one first and it was a gold BMX. I picked up a heavy one, it was a Nintendo Wii!

ADAM CULLEN (11)

Alderman White School & Language College, Bramcote

HUNTING FOR DEATH

Jack and his friends would go hunting for fun. One night he went alone. This trip was going to be a long and unforgettable one. When Jack arrived he noticed the forest was very dim and cold. After a couple of hours, Jack heard loud thunder coming towards him …

BAKOR AL-AMRY (14)

Alderman White School & Language College, Bramcote

UNTITLED

Once upon a time the bells rang out for Santa, and Sam Crosby wrapped up a present for CJ. It was an exploding jack-in-a-box and CJ had stars in his eyes.

'Wow! what a cool present. I'm so happy!'
Everyone had a very merry, happy Christmas!

CONNOR HARRISON (12)

Alderman White School & Language College, Bramcote

THE TEXT MESSAGE

Amy was going to babysit when her friends came
over to help her. Amy got a text message. It was
from someone called the teaser.
'Amy has a boyfriend,' said Dannie.
The message said, 'I'm watching you. Lock the
doors and windows now!'

LUCY KENDALL (11)
Alderman White School & Language College, Bramcote

THE HOUSE

Smoke rises from the chimney, flashes of faces run across windows … No human lives there but something does. Stabs of pain down my leg when peering at the house. Ghostly figures lurking by the door. Cracks in the windows suddenly appear. What lives there? I am going to find out … Now!

NIKITA COPE (12)

Alderman White School & Language College, Bramcote

THE UNSOLVABLE MYSTERY

Driving to the scene of unsolvable crime,
headlamps shining bright, I could see a body.
Sounds of swords and screams! 'Who's there?'
No reply. Looked around, ran to the car.
Someone was following me; I slammed my foot
down, drove away. Looked at my side - someone
was there.

THOMAS MACSWEENEY (12)
Alderman White School & Language College, Bramcote

THE POOL

A man at the swimming pool was pulled in. Next
day, same thing happened.
Next day a man at the pool with a rope around
his waist got pulled in, got pulled out covered in
green slime.
They drained the pool and found a dead monster,
there since time's dawn.

LUCY TURNER (12)

Alderman White School & Language College, Bramcote

POSH GIRL

I live on an estate with my best friends. They are
common. I am very posh. My mum detests them.
I think, *I have to teach them manners and speech.*
Wow! They say, 'How are you Mrs Brand?'
Soo, it's the moment of truth. My mum loves
them! It's great.

DAISY RAYNOR (11)

Alderman White School & Language College, Bramcote

SHOPLIFTER

A sixteen-year-old boy kept shoplifting and the shopkeeper had been to prison fifteen times for murder. So after he got fed up with the boy robbing, he decided to get his own back and chased him.
Nobody knew what happened but the boy was found dead. Shopkeeper smiled.

WILLDAN COOMBES (12)

Alderman White School & Language College, Bramcote

NIGHTMARE HOLIDAY

This is a story from my nightmare holiday, supposed to be the best holiday. My first time on a plane went terribly wrong. A flash, everyone dead, except me. I checked everywhere to see what caused it. I saw nothing. I gazed through the window, a shadowy shape loomed outside ...

MICHAEL THOMAS (12)

Alderman White School & Language College, Bramcote

39

CREAK!

It was 2am and pitch-black when I heard the stairs creak. Who was there? I was sure I was alone. I sat bolt upright. Every creak got louder, they were coming up the stairs. My heart was pounding, threatening to break out. The figure burst in and …

ELEANOR BEESTIN (11)

Alderman White School & Language College, Bramcote

TEACHERS

Teachers … God they're boring … Mrs Helm
speaking French all the time. Mr Keeling always
blabbing on and Mr Moore, a maths lesson and
yet he talks about, 'Back in the day …'
I hate this stuff, these lessons, this place. It's like
Hell. Ya know what? I wanna go bed dude.

RYAN DICKIN (12)

Ash Field School, Leicester

41

TIME TRAVEL ADVENTURE

It was another normal weekend. I was playing on my Nintendo. I decided to watch a film, then I came up with a brilliant idea. I would build a time machine! And I did. When I had finished, I got in, travelled time and got back home.

WASEEM SALEEM (11)
Ash Field School, Leicester

WHEN I BROKE MY ARM

One Saturday afternoon, playing football on the
trampoline, I was in goal. I made a huge save and
hit my hand on a metal pole. I fell and cried. I
shouted for Dad.
'It's only bruised,' he said.
One week later I was taken to hospital with a
broken bone!

JASON BARNFATHER (11)

Ash Field School, Leicester

GOODBYE BULLIES

Walking back after a daunting day at school, creeping past the trees, knowing someone is gonna hurt me. They are here. Oh no! I don't wanna get hurt this time. They're looking at me as if they're gonna kill me! There's a rope. I should, I will …
Goodbye bullies!

LYDIA DUCKWORTH (12)

Friesland School, Nottingham

DEATH IN THE OFFICE

The desk was empty; the papers untouched. The
brother and sister stepped cautiously into the
deserted office, shivering at the cold wind from
the shattered window, rustling papers. The door
slammed behind them, causing the whole room
to shudder. The demon headmaster, sleeves
rolled up, laughed menacingly. Sudden death!

MEGAN GODBER (12)

Friesland School, Nottingham

THE CHAOTIC CHRISTMAS

Christmas! At last it's here. I ran to wake up
Jodie. She wouldn't wake up. Then *stomp, stomp,
stomp!* I wasn't the only one up! I ran to Mum
and Dad's room, they weren't there! I ran back
to Jodie's room. She wasn't there either! Maybe
they'll come back soon.

HOLLY BERESFORD (11)

Friesland School, Nottingham

LOST TOM

One day Tom was skateboarding and saw some vandals, damaging a boy's bike. Tom said to himself, 'Thank God I did not bring my bike, it would've been damaged.'
One of the vandals saw Tom. He had an idea - when Tom got out he was knocked out bad style.

AKASH SINGH (11)

Friesland School, Nottingham

PE TRAUMA

Hop, skip, jump! It's PE today. I hate PE. I'm gonna scream. I think I'd better get involved before I get told off. Run! Run! I'm running to catch the ball. *Splat!* I'm on my back. Pete runs to Miss.

Miss runs over to me. 'Are you OK?'
'I'm fine!'

BETSYMAE KIRKLAND-BALL (11)
Friesland School, Nottingham

THE DAY THE EARTH WAS SILENT

One sunny day I was walking along the beach but then, the sun went down. It was freezing. I was scared. I heard a sound like ghosts. I walked home. When I stepped in, nobody was there. The lights were off, the doors closed. Something touched me. What was it?

MONICA GHENT (11)

Friesland School, Nottingham

UNTITLED

Home alone for the first time. I have thirty minutes, what can I do in thirty minutes? There's a bang upstairs. *What was that?* I think. I creep up the stairs, looking behind me constantly. My wardrobe's rumbling, I open the doors to my wardrobe and then suddenly …

RACHEL SCOTT (11)

Friesland School, Nottingham

REAL NAMES! REAL LIFE

'Oh, I can't finish my mini saga for Mr Mercer,'
Ryan said.
'Leave it,' said Charlie.
'Yes, done!' Ryan shouted. Even though he knew
it was pants, he still sent it off.
The next day Ryan got home to find a letter. It
read, 'You're in the book!'.
'Yes! Ha!'

RYAN GRUNDY (11)
Friesland School, Nottingham

A YOUNG FOOTBALLER

'Joe, hurry up or you're gonna be late for
football!' shouted Joe's mum.
'OK,' he replied.
Joe got there and to his surprise the manager of
his favourite football team, Glasgow Rangers, was
there.
'Oh what?' said Joe, gobsmacked. He played his
best and he was scouted. 'Yes, perfect day!'

JACK NICHOLSON (11)

Friesland School, Nottingham

THE GHOSTLY CAR

I once saw a car driving down the road, but the scary thing was, that the car had no driver! I stopped to look at it and when I saw the side of it, I saw a small, tiny person driving it, just managing to look over the steering wheel.

ALEXANDER MENZIES (11)

Friesland School, Nottingham

I SAW A DRAGON

I was alone in my ancient house, surrounded by a tremendous orchard. Suddenly I heard another knock on the creaky, wooden door. I fell back and rubbed my hands on the rusty piano, searching for a way out. Then it appeared! Rainbow-scales, anchored-tail, I knew what it was …

ISAAC JESSON (12)

Friesland School, Nottingham

MONSTER FROM BELOW

Lucy wasn't a disrespectful girl, that's what
everyone thought. She was a monster. But this
monster was about to be obliterated. There was
a ferocious being waiting for her, ready to tear
her limb from limb.
She stepped up to the door, something bellowed
ferociously, 'Lucy, tidy your room now!'

DANIEL WALDER (11)
Friesland School, Nottingham

MAD SCIENTIST

A scientist, driven mad by failed experiments, was trying to create life. His creation blew up, burning him. It set him on fire, but he did not die, he kept on burning. The strange thing was, it didn't hurt him. So this mad scientist, ever burning, decided to fight crime.

CHARLIE MACNAMEE (11)

Friesland School, Nottingham

THE BRAIN

One day in Oddsberg Dr Frankenstein was operating on patients who wanted their hair cutting. Hours later a patient went up to him and said, 'A bit off the top please.'
Later that evening he noticed that his brain was missing!
Next day he kept shouting, 'Where is my brain?'

ANDREW JOHNSON (11)

Friesland School, Nottingham

FIREFLIES

Long ago lived three witches called Hat, Mat and
Fred and they had children called Flat, Spat and
Fat. They lived in an underground volcano. It was
infested by fireflies. No ordinary fireflies. The flies
were on fire and everything burned down to lots
of hot smelly ash.

GEORGE BEECHING (11)

Friesland School, Nottingham

FRIEND'S TRUST

I had a friend called Chanel, until one day she shouted at me and hit me. As she ripped my skin apart, I told her to stop. I thought to myself, *she is meant to be my friend.* Then I hit her back. She was the worst friend I'd had.

KATIE STUBBS (11)
Friesland School, Nottingham

SHADOW IN THE DARKNESS

Emma ripped off her pyjamas and crept into the dark, cold lake. She swam to the middle feeling the coldness hitting her body painfully. Suddenly she spotted a long, dark shadow beneath her, and before she knew it, it grabbed her leg, pulling her rapidly under the calm water ... *crocodile!*

EVIE DARNELL (11)

Friesland School, Nottingham

ARGH!

Argh! As I stepped out of bed, I looked in the mirror to find I was bald. I rushed downstairs, there was silence. Alone and afraid, I tried to call Mum, the phone was dead! Then all of a sudden a bony hand tapped my shoulder, Mum was back!

CHERISH JOHNSON (11)

Friesland School, Nottingham

THE POORLY LEOPARD

Once there was a tiger, his name was Leo. He had a friend but his friend was in hospital. He was a leopard who had a broken foot. He had a lot of friends visiting him, so the tiger didn't get noticed. So in the end he left him.

KATI HUTCHINGS (11)

Friesland School, Nottingham

THE THING

It was horrid, six eyes, three legs and countless
fingers. Ten million heads - some had no eyes,
because there were only six of them. It was as
wide as Birmingham and as tall as the Empire
State Building. Don't get me started on the size of
its feet! 'Hello Steve.'

DOUGLAS NEWHAM (11)
Friesland School, Nottingham

63

THE OLYMPICS

Walking down a long, narrow hallway, I see
the light creep trough the gap in the door and
suddenly, *flash!* A crowd of people cheer and
shout as I enter the stadium. The pool, the track,
trampoline, rowing, long jump, diving, archery.
Here I am at the Olympic Games!

CHARLOTTE HOPGOOD (11)

Friesland School, Nottingham

THINGS GO BUMP IN THE NIGHT

I woke in the night to strange noises. I got out of bed to see what was in my bedroom, it was clear. I went downstairs and it got louder. I went into the kitchen. Something scratched my foot. I turned the light on, it was the cat. *Miaow!*

CURT EVISON (11)
Friesland School, Nottingham

UNTITLED

'Mum!' shouted James, whilst lying in bed at
twelve. His mum came running to the room.
'What's wrong?'
James replied anxiously, 'I saw a ghost!'
His mum said, 'I'm sure it's just your imagination.'
'No, I'm not joking, it was a real ghost.'
Bang! It came from downstairs, they screamed.

MATT COBB (12)

Friesland School, Nottingham

SAKURA (CHERRY BLOSSOM)

Sakura falls like soft snow. He waits, American, blue eyes. His love approaches, heart fluttering under her obi. A white and red mask hides her blush. He smiles and holds out his hand. A black blur, scorned lover, katana in hand. The blade sharp. Blue eyes fall. Their dream ends.

EMMA SABIN (16)

John Leggott Sixth Form College, Scunthorpe

SURPRISINGLY BRIGHT PINK

Bang! I was on the moon. It was beyond my
expectations. It was a surprisingly bright pink
colour. Was I dreaming?
It wasn't until a spaceship landed near to me that
I knew there was a way out. But in my mind I
wondered, would I ever get home?

PHILIPPA MARSHALL (16)

John Leggott Sixth Form College, Scunthorpe

UNTITLED

Sometimes it's hard to think of ideas off the top of your head. Sometimes it's scary being put on the spot. Sometimes it's good to try new things. Sometimes we judge things before we try them. Sometimes it's good to go to bed late. Sometimes we laugh for no reason.

NIKKI THOMPSON (17)

John Leggott Sixth Form College, Scunthorpe

THE PREY

I saw it coming towards me, staring at me with its fierce eyes. Its hawk-like beak ready to cut through my flesh. It came closer and closer as my heart beat faster with every second. Then, *splat!* The bird smashed itself against the windscreen of my car. Silly bird!

NAYAAB REINA PATHAN (14)

Judgemeadow Community College, Leicester

BUTTERFLIES IN MY STOMACH

Johnny's parents never took him to the zoo or circus. They told him that all animals should roam free. On the morning of his first day at school, Johnny was found covered in blood. He'd slit his own stomach. Somehow he recovered.
'I had butterflies in my stomach!' he explained.

MUBBASSIR TALATI (12)

Judgemeadow Community College, Leicester

71

LIFE STORY

Cut out of my mum's belly. Went to primary school. Sat on a splinter. Went to hospital. Popped out, finished primary school. Went to comp. Fell off the stage in a play. Got beat up by Jake. Leaving school soon. What do you think will happen next?

JAKE RADFORD (13)
Kimberley School, Kimberley

THE FLYING MOTORCYCLE

On a night like no other, a man had just invented
the first flying motorcycle. As he started the
engine, it roared like a lion defending its cubs.
The bike lifted off the ground with the man at its
handles. Suddenly the bike fell with the man on it.
Splat!

DANIEL SWIFT (12)

Kimberley School, Kimberley

SCISSORS

I was eagerly swept into the chair. 'Get it off. I
want it all off.'
The scissors came towards my head. Gnashing
away, they got closer. The man looked at my head
like a ravenous dog.
I looked in the mirror. 'Nice hair, thanks!' I said.

NATALIE POXON (13)

Kimberley School, Kimberley

THE BEAST

As I looked up at the putrid-smelling beast, its beady eyes were still glaring at me. Its hair was scruffy and dry like straw. Its teeth stuck out and were covered in mouldy meat. This is why I don't like coming here to the teachers' staffroom.

SEAN O'DOWD (13)
Kimberley School, Kimberley

HIS CAVE

As I cautiously open the door of the cave, the first thing that hits me is the odour. Green gases drifting around me. I grasp something to shield my nose. But what is it? *Ewww!* Malodorous, grey boxers! I sprint out. I will never venture into my brother's room again.

FRANCES EYRE (12)

Kimberley School, Kimberley

VICTORY IS CLOSE

There it was, the dark figure, lurking in the corner. I had my eyes on it everywhere it went. I pulled out my handgun. I got my finger on the trigger. I was ready to shoot. I shot. *Bullseye!* I got him. The game of Laser Quest was over.

OLIVER SKINNER (11)
Kimberley School, Kimberley

FIGHT!

Standing there, terrified. I really shouldn't be
standing in this crowd, but I'm desperate to know
what happens next. She briefly glances at me,
her face fuming with anger. She turns around
and slaps her opponent to the ground. I stand in
shock. My best friend is now a monster.

ALICIA MARTIN-JONES (13)

Kimberley School, Kimberley

THE CUP

The silence had broken. He stormed down the left wing with the ball. The tension was crazy. If he scored this, we'd win the cup. The goalkeeper was setting himself for the shot. It was silent …

Goal! He scored!

'Sam! Breakfast!'

It was just a dream. Hope Chelsea win!

SCOTT TAYLOR (12)

Kimberley School, Kimberley

79

BEFORE DEATH

My eyes blurred slowly, as my deep infected wound bubbled blood. My breath deepened. A low voice, howling, darkness overpowering me as my body slowly died. My skin as pale as snow. I struggled slowly but I knew it was the end. I was gone.

MATTHEW KEADY (12)

Kimberley School, Kimberley

THE THINGS THAT LURK IN THE ROOM!

Dad cut the carcass to pieces. There was steam in the room, the horrid smell was awful. Green things were slithering but something drowned out the horrible smell. It was thick, sloppy and brown. Sunday dinner was gorgeous and yummy.

NATASHA GAMBLE (11)

Kimberley School, Kimberley

THE WITCH IN THE KITCHEN

I picked the slimy grey slugs off my pizza. I took a bite, cheese oozing through my teeth, wrapping round my throat like a spider's web. Blood-red sauce burnt my tongue. The witch had made up the most poisonous meal yet. I'm not stopping school dinners tomorrow.

ELLIE BROWN (12)

Kimberley School, Kimberley

PASSION, FEAR, ISOLATION

Left, right, where should I go? I ran, sprinted.
They were coming for me. The rain poured, I
stumbled, I was trapped in a large enclosed place.
Tick-tock, tick-tock. Five, four, three, two, one -
Bang! Everything stood till for a second. *Goal!* The
left back stopped chasing me.

ELLIS CAREY (12)
Kimberley School, Kimberley

MY UNLUCKY FALL

It began slowly. However, it quickly sped up and soon I fell off and rolled down the slope, ice cutting me. The sledge was gone. I somehow ended up in front of another sledger and as he swerved to avoid me, I hit the bottom of the toboggan slope!

SCOTT STANDEN (12)

Kimberley School, Kimberley

HOUSE

The deserted black wreck lay torn and damaged.
The burnt ancient panels of the once upstairs
bedroom. My eyes fixed and red. A garden wall
rotting and moulding slowly. A shiver of fear
vibrated quickly throughout the ruins. A lone
beast waiting. A house, my house.

MATTHEW KEADY (12)

Kimberley School, Kimberley

CHRISTMAS COOKIES

Christmas Eve … I just can't sleep! Maybe if I
go get something to eat I'll fall asleep. I creep
downstairs to find someone eating the cookies
left for Santa. 'Oh my God! It's Santa!'
'Shh, be quiet Ellie! You'll wake the whole house!'
'Dad, why are you eating Santa's cookies?'

RUBY PERSAUD (12)

Kimberley School, Kimberley

A DAY IN A FRAGILE MIND

A small, dark room, me sitting in the middle, my legs pressed to my chest. Tears falling from my eyes. My broken heart, so fragile and beautiful. Glistening eyes with such a story to tell. A drop of rich, thick, red liquid fell heavily onto my cold shaking hand. Blood!

LAURIE STALEY (12)

Kimberley School, Kimberley

MRS SMILEY

My mum's maiden name was Smiley. She said she liked it because she was always happy not to be married. Then one day she met my dad, Mr Grumps. Now she says she's always grumpy because she's married. She also says marriage is not a word, it's a sentence.

REBECCA CHAPMAN (12)

Kimberley School, Kimberley

ICE SCREAM VAN

I was walking home from my friend's house when all of a sudden a white van approached me. It began to play a scary tune. It skidded past me and stopped. My heart sank. I was terrified. The window opened, a man leaned out and said, 'Want an ice cream?'

JOHN KING (13)
Kimberley School, Kimberley

ROBIN THE HOOD

'Quick Edward, our jewels have been stolen from
our teak cabinet,' yelled the posh lady.
'Right, us posher upper class people are getting
targeted by the devious Robin Hood!'
Meanwhile Robin Hood was at the pawn brokers
collecting his cash from the previous night's theft.
'Here you go,' whispered John.

JAMES HEESOM (13)

Kimberley School, Kimberley

THE TICKLE MONSTER

Tears rolled down Ria's face. 'Please don't!' she shouted. She tried to escape. Sweat was running down her face and dripping to the ground. She fell to the ground and tried to slap him away. He grinned. She grinned. He began to tickle her again. She screamed at him!

SOPHIE WADSLEY (12)

Kimberley School, Kimberley

A LOVE STORY

He was handsome. She was really pretty. 'I met
him in Lou-Lou's café.'
'I saw her in the corner of Lou-Lou's café.'
'I couldn't stop staring at him.'
'I couldn't help but look at her.'
It was from that day on we knew we would be
together forever.

MOLLIE EVANS (12)

Kimberley School, Kimberley

THE RACE

My palms were sweaty, my heart beating. The starting gun echoed around the stadium. The track was becoming blurry, the stands seemed to be getting smaller. Thousands of faces in a confined space, just the thought was sending me dizzy. An enormous roar erupted from the crowd. I had won!

CASSIE BLAGDEN (13)
Kimberley School, Kimberley

THE DEVIL IN THE DARK

I heard the noise again. This time much louder. My heart was racing, echoing inside me, in a perfect rhythm. I turned rapidly, trying to work out the dark room in disguise. I wanted to move, but my feet felt like they were cemented to the floor. I was trapped …

ELLA GAYLE (13)

Kimberley School, Kimberley

ESCAPING

It stood silently, signalling the others to be aware, and then it galloped. The others followed, sensing they were all in great danger, but not knowing what from. They galloped towards the horizon, leaving heavy hoof prints in the crust of the ground. They had escaped, leaving the predator behind.

HOLLY ALLARD (12)
Kimberley School, Kimberley

THE SNAKE SCARE

Ellis had a pet snake. He absolutely adored it.
One day Ellis went to clean it out, when he
noticed his snake wasn't moving. He picked it
up and to his horror noticed it wasn't breathing
either. He turned round and realised it was only
the snake's shed skin!

BETHANY THOMAS (12)

Kimberley School, Kimberley

HURT

The children looked out the murky window and wondered what would happen when he walked through the door. She held the baby tight in her arms, scared of what might happen next. A tear rolled from her eye as she whispered softly to the baby, 'One day we'll be free.'

OLIVIA MARSHALL (12)
Kimberley School, Kimberley

TOOTH FAIRY

I was asleep, something in the night awoke me. I turned over to face the creature. As it got closer I saw a hand come out to reach me. The hand slid under my pillow and grabbed whatever was under there, replacing it with a coin. It was my mother!

HANNAH HAZLEDINE (13)

Kimberley School, Kimberley

SUMMER LOVING

As summer was coming to an end, Joe and I attempted our second kiss; the first had ended in a headbutt. As our lips locked, my worst nightmare came true - my phone rang! It was my mother! Not the kiss I had been hoping for.

BECKIE O'DOUD & NICOLE BOTTS (13)

Kimberley School, Kimberley

DEAD FAIRY

The night came quicker than she thought. She fluttered out of Tooth Fairy Land to swap two pounds for Catlin's tooth. She glided through the window and landed gracefully on the bed. As she crept under the pillow, Catlin rolled over and squished her.

DEMI-LEA FALKNER (13)

Kimberley School, Kimberley

SPOT THE BALL

Saturday afternoon - Man U v Arsenal. Rooney ran towards goal, the shot was in the air. What happened? Where's the ball? It turned out Rooney had hit it so hard that no one could see it until it hit Colleen Rooney in the face. *Ouch!*

RYAN BAKER (13)
Kimberley School, Kimberley

THE CIRCUS

I stepped into the big top, where animals danced,
orchestras played, ringleader ordered. He
blew his whistle and the clowns drove out in a
small white car covered in multicoloured spots.
Suddenly a large rocky volcano erupted into the
circus and scared people everywhere.
My imaginary world was completely destroyed.

LEWIS SWAIN (13)
Kimberley School, Kimberley

CLOSE QUARTERS

He came at me. I pulled the slide back on my
M4. I placed my last round in it. His AK was
jammed but he charged me with it bayoneted.
My crosshairs rested between his eyes. Coolly
I squeezed the trigger. He flung back. Brains
covered the walls and floor.

CHARLIE MILLINGTON (13)

Kimberley School, Kimberley

THE MONSTER'S CAVERN

The cavern was dimly lit, and the only sound was the dripping of the gargantuan's saliva splashing on the floor. But where was it? Then it came … a giant roar screamed from the thick walls of the cave, had he heard me? With the sword tightly gripped, I marched forward.

JONATHON LANGFORD (13)

Kimberley School, Kimberley

GUN

It's not just the metal you touch on a gun. It's the whisper of death. I held the weapon to his head. I could see pleading in his eyes. I knew to succeed I could not hesitate. I pulled the trigger, white filled my eyes ... Game completed.

NOAH SUGARMAN (11)

Kimberley School, Kimberley

THE BUTCHER

I couldn't do it, but I had to. I sliced the knife through the skin, the blood oozed out. I penetrated through the bone with the knife then sliced him up. I finally finished it, the gore was over. The beef was ready to go in the oven.

DALE MATTHEWS (11)

Kimberley School, Kimberley

THE NIGHT BEFORE CHRISTMAS

The night before Christmas. I love Christmas. I can't go to sleep. I'll try and go to sleep. I'm going to sleep now, goodnight. Oh I can't go to sleep, I'm going downstairs. I can hear noises. Oh my goodness, it's Santa. I rammed the door open ... it's Dad!

KAMALDEEP KAUR (13)

Kimberley School, Kimberley

THIRD PLACE

Three, two, one, go! I, in my rather gorgeous car, start the race. I'm overtaken by a strange mushroom guy. Second place. *Bam!* I'm overtaken by a blonde girl with a glittering crown. The final lap and I'm in third. It's all over. Third place. I hate 'Mario Kart DS'.

ELEANOR SHAW (13)

Kimberley School, Kimberley

SECONDS TO GO

Swirling, rocking, round in circles. Grabbing for
the boat, getting dangerously close to the current.
The Eclipse is already caught in it. Splashing water
into the other boats. Water levels are dropping
increasingly, pulling us closer to the dreaded hole.
But then it's gone, water and whirlpool. The
bath's empty!

MEGAN HAYMAN TANSLEY (12)

Kimberley School, Kimberley

109

FOLLOWED

As I was strolling home, there was a green car
following me! Every time I turned a corner it
followed. Soon I came to a dead end. No way
out! Suddenly a man appeared out of the car. It
was my neighbour. 'Do you want a lift?'

SOPHIE HAY (13)
Kimberley School, Kimberley

THE CHASE

It was pitch-black. The chase was on. What had I done? Yet the chase went on faster and faster down the dark, murky street. Past lamp post after lamp post. Why were they chasing me? I turned around and it was Mark on his bike. 'I got you, good!'

DANIEL KNOWLES (13)

Kimberley School, Kimberley

SNAKE ESCAPE

I panted, the vicious, yellow, twelve-metre snake slid across the sand. My feet were sinking. Could I make it? The shelter was just in sight, but I could see the snake out of the corner of my eye, creeping closer behind me. I turned the page. I'd finished it!

ELLIE BATES (12)

Kimberley School, Kimberley

CRASH! BANG! GAME OVER

The brake was jammed, the view was blurry as I drifted around the corner. The crash barrier came closer to my view. It shattered my windscreen. All I could see was blood. My vision flashed. Game over! Enter more credit!

AIMÉE PROCTOR (12)

Kimberley School, Kimberley

THE RED BUTTON

President Bush sat in his office watching television, when his phone rang. He lifted up the handset and brought it to his ear. 'I understand. Goodbye.' He took a slender silver remote off his desk. His finger stabbed down on a red button. The TV listings popped onto the screen!

WILLIAM SAUNDERS (13)

Kimberley School, Kimberley

DOB!

Running through the busy town, I pant and look behind myself. Oh no, he's right there, I'll be behind bars forever. Even though it wasn't my fault. I have to keep running.

'Dob! You're It!' Great! Now I've got to chase him back!

RUBY POYNTER (12)

Kimberley School, Kimberley

A MODERN CINDERELLA

My name is Cindy and my dad's banged up,
right. So I was living with this weirdo I called
my stepmum until … I met this well fit lad, P
Charming, at a disco. At this disco my Nike fell
off. So he gave it me back. Now we are hitched.

MEGAN KEETLEY (14)
Kimberley School, Kimberley

TRAGEDY

Pain, anger, sorrow. Moses looked at the pale
bodies sprawled in front of him. Dead. Just
minutes before, this car was full of love and joy.
'Are we nearly there yet?'
'I'm hungry!'
'I can't wait!'
The car was a Concorde, speeding towards
Heaven. A lorry?
'Mum ... watch out!'

AMELIA MARRON (13)
Kimberley School, Kimberley

TRENCHES

The guns had stopped. I turned to see my comrades. Their faces drenched in fear, but buried somewhere in their emotions there was curiosity. Curiosity killed the cat, but will it kill the Tommy?
My men were ready. Men? Not even old enough to buy a beer! The whistle blew …

BEN SWINN (13)

Kimberley School, Kimberley

NEEDLES

I went in. I sat down. The stencil was on. I couldn't go back now. I was curious. I looked in the mirror. Agreed. The needle hit, the pain hit, it was like being punched by a heavy-weight boxer. Two hours. Done. 'Wow!' I said. 'What a great tattoo!'

JESSICA SILVERS (13)

Kimberley School, Kimberley

SHADOWS

Mayzee remembered her mother's stern words
before she left the house. 'Whatever you do
Mayzee, do not step in the shadows!'
She reached the baker's shop and paid for the
bread. She stepped out of the building. The
sun had gone down and there were shadows
everywhere. She was stuck!

MEGAN HOWELL (12)

King Edward VII School, Melton Mowbray

TWINKLE TWINKLE LITTLE STAR, MY VIEW

It's a clear night, the moon is bright and I shine up above the world so bright, like a diamond in the sky. I shine, twinkling all night, being watched, gazed at by mysterious creatures like a TV. How famous am I? The sun rises. I go down. Good morning!

ZAK MISIUDA (12)

King Edward VII School, Melton Mowbray

LONELY

It was a sunny day, I was at the park on the swing.
My friend had just left. I was all alone. I was just
sitting still on the swing. Suddenly there was
a gust of wind. It felt like the spirits from the
graveyard arose to haunt me.

RACHEL FOSTER (13)
King Edward VII School, Melton Mowbray

THE HOUSE

There is a horrifying house at the bottom of the
street. It's believed to be haunted.
Tom was out alone at night. When he walked past
the house. He decided to go inside. He opened
the door, it creaked. It closed by itself - and never
opened again …

ALICIA PATEL (13)

King Edward VII School, Melton Mowbray

LITTLE PINK RIDING HOOD

Ashley rang me and asked me if I could go over as she was feeling unwell. I was skipping through the woods when a wolf jumped out and asked me where I was going.
When I got there Ashley was gone. All I could see was a shadow creep past …

LAURA FAIRBROTHER (12)

King Edward VII School, Melton Mowbray

OLIVIA'S TRAGEDY

Olivia walked home and saw her garage was open
and no car inside. She went and shut her garage
and went inside her dark house. She saw her
mum sitting on the couch. 'Mum, where's Dad?'
'He's left us!'
'But why?'
Her mum sniffed.
'Mum, why?'
'You know exactly why!'

LIBBIE BENNETT (13)
King Edward VII School, Melton Mowbray

TOM'S WALK HOME

Tom was walking home from school. He felt tired and was half asleep. Suddenly he heard an old footstep. He looked around, there was an old man sitting on a wall. He fell off. Tom went over. The old man was dead. Tom ran and ran and ran!

MICHAEL BROWN (14)

King Edward VII School, Melton Mowbray

SMALL HANDS, BIG RESPONSIBILITY

This is how it began - a sword in a stone, pulled out by young hands, used to defeat strong enemies. Although he was a child, the gods trusted him with ultimate power and a big responsibility. As he became adult, the enemies became truly stronger until it was the end …

SAM SNODIN (13)

King Edward VII School, Melton Mowbray

THE POST BOX BEASTIE

Timmy walked up to the post box. Suddenly a slimy hand shot out and grabbed his cuff. He tried to struggle but it overpowered him. It dragged him into the post box, then with a squelch it ate him. There was a pause, it waited and prepared to feast.

OLIVER DALBY (12)
King Edward VII School, Melton Mowbray

MARY HAD A LITTLE LAMB

I bought a little lamb and his fleece was white as the snow on the ground, but the bad thing was he followed me wherever I went. Even when I went to school. Although he's always there and I never get any peace and quiet, I love having him there!

CHLOE I'ANSON (12)
King Edward VII School, Melton Mowbray

THE SPLIT

Something felt uneasy when Abbie walked downstairs to greet her parents in the morning. Not a word was spoken, murmured silence wasn't golden. Abbie's parents sat her down to tell her the saddening news. 'We have decided to break up. We're sorry, we can't live together anymore. We're getting divorced!'

EMILY CRAGG (15)
King Edward VII School, Melton Mowbray

MY LLAMA

I had a pet llama. He was called Roosevelt. I took
him to the farmer, now my llama is no more. My
llama now is sold in McDonald's with his mummy
and daddy and all of his cousins. Why'd I give my
llama to the farmer? He'd still be alive.

LOUISE WELLS (14)
King Edward VII School, Melton Mowbray

ALFIE'S CHOICE

There was a slight clammy feeling in the shop. Beads of sweat were trickling down Alfie's forehead. Tension and suspense were building. Which one? Suddenly he realised that he had been losing concentration. He understood which newspaper he would buy but which chocolate bar would he choose? Snickers or Mars?

JACK LAUGHTON (14)

King Edward VII School, Melton Mowbray

MAKE A SENTENCE USING FASCINATE

'Emily can go.'
'I went to the zoo and was fascinated.'
'Almost, how about Jack?'
'I went to the museum, it was fascinating.'
'Nearly, Jimmy you can go.'
'My gran got a cardigan for Christmas with ten
buttons but because her boobs were too big, she
could only fasten eight.'

TOM JINKS (15)
King Edward VII School, Melton Mowbray

TRAMP

The car was speeding down the slip road. One wheel lifted from the ground. The car landed but in the process nailed an eighty-year-old tramp, who had lived his life in misery because of his bird that died when he was nine. The car was a Vauxhall.

THOMAS JONES (14)

King Edward VII School, Melton Mowbray

FOREVER RUNNING

Running and fast. Praying to God that they wouldn't catch me. I had to run - from my past, from every mistake I'd ever made. How long could I keep going? Suddenly it woke up. Was this what was to become of me? Would I be running for my whole life?

RYAN MARTIN (15)

King Edward VII School, Melton Mowbray

THE ANGEL

One day, when Emmett was backpacking he found a bear. The bear liked the smell of Emmett, so he attacked. Then the bear ran away and Emmett saw her - the angel, with golden eyes and hair. He felt something besides pain. Love. Then she picked him up and ran away …

LUCY STARBUCK (14)

King Edward VII School, Melton Mowbray

MY MINI SAGA

I had waited years for this moment. 'Not long now,' I told myself. My heart raced as I climbed into my spacesuit. My hands were clammy. *I can't turn back now.* I took a deep breath. Ready? Ten, nine, eight, seven, six, five, four, three, two, one, lift-off!

NICOLA MEDHURST (14)

King Edward VII School, Melton Mowbray

THE CHASE

I was running, faster than I ever had before.
Wind blowing into my sweaty face, my hair
trailing along behind me, slowing me down. I
had to get away from the monsters chasing me.
Suddenly one of them pulled me down on to the
playground. The bullies had succeeded again.

CHARLIE PERRIAM (15)

King Edward VII School, Melton Mowbray

BRUNO

The worst day of my life. Mum came home and it was there. Scared and nervous I went to see it. I've never seen an alien before! It had twenty beady eyes, staring at me. It was the weirdest thing I've ever seen.
'Darling, this is your baby brother, Bruno.'

ELEANOR WENBORN (14)

King Edward VII School, Melton Mowbray

THE BEGINNING OF THE BOY WHO NEVER GREW UP

It was a cold, crisp November night when I found him there. It was a strange sight, a child alone, especially so late at night. I couldn't leave him there, not by himself anyway. I took him home. There he became known as Peter Pan. Me, I'm called Tink!

SALLYANN FOSTER (14)

King Edward VII School, Melton Mowbray

MY DEATH

'Argh!' I screamed. The knife was to my throat, blood dripped from my neck, making puddles on the floor. I shouted but nobody heard. The knife lunged deeper into my throat. The last scream hurt. My heart pounding, 'Just a dream,' I whispered. Sweat dripped off my face.

EMILY EDWARDS (12)

Newbridge High School, Coalville

GOAL 3! BACK TO ENGLAND

The score's two-one to Everton with five minutes to go. Liverpool require a win to secure the cup. Alonso scores a thumper! Two-all. It isn't enough. They demand another. Gerrard's gone down! It's a penalty! Gerrard needs to score! *Wham!* Off the crossbar. It's in. Liverpool - English champions.

SAM KRYWIUK (12)
Newbridge High School, Coalville

THE NIGHT BEFORE THE WEDDING

I went down for dinner the night before the
wedding. They emptied the restaurant for me.
Then I went down to the beach. I stormed back
to the hotel.
The morning awoke me and I got dressed and
walked down the isle. Gary ran from the church.
Were we married?

KIRSTY SAVORY (12)

Newbridge High School, Coalville

UNTITLED

I was spinning out of control. Bright light flashed before my eyes. I gripped my seat. A cold sweat on my back, my hair plastered to my head. Faster, faster, faster. My eyes wide and bloodshot with fear.

The 'Teapot' is the scariest ride in the world!

ISABELLE BEESTON (13)

Newbridge High School, Coalville

HEAR THE CRY

In silence I stood.
He wailed, 'Hand out!' looking straight at me. He
brought the cane back.
I squeezed my eyes tight. My hand went out.
Swoosh! Mary Smith howled. *Phew,* I thought he
was going to hit me!

PAIGE MCWILLIAM (13)
Newbridge High School, Coalville

THE HUNT

A dark shape slowly swims towards a playful seal.
Its dorsal fin slices through the ocean spray like
a glinting knife on a circular dinner plate. The
creature tenses, poised for attack. It's too late
now … it lunges! The seal escapes. Returning to
land, it looks back. Jaws can wait …

ZOE BLINKO (13)
Newbridge High School, Coalville

FROZEN WATER

It looked under the water, stalking its poor prey.
I stood there. Frozen, awaiting the inevitable
violent assault from this unforgiving abomination.
The water was stone-cold, just like the creature's
heart … it honed in on its prey and *snap!* The fish
was caught on a hook! What a catch!

DAVID SLEIGH (13)

Newbridge High School, Coalville

FOUND YOU!

I sat there, curled up in a sphere behind the sofa.
I could hear footsteps getting closer. There was
gasping and more footsteps. I sat there, as silent
as I could. It was in the same room as me! It was
now towering over me.

'Found you!' roared Lilly, comically.

ABI BICKNELL (13)
Newbridge High School, Coalville

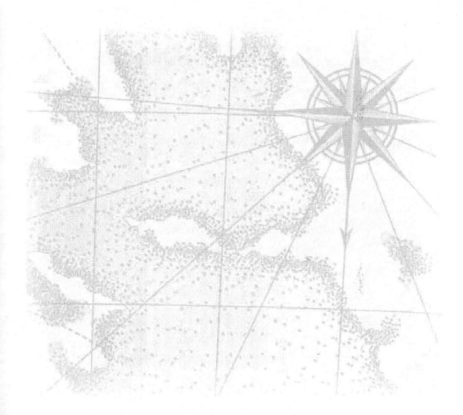

INFORMATION

We hope you have enjoyed reading this book - and that you will continue to enjoy it in the coming years.

If you like reading and writing, drop us a line or give us a call and we'll send you a free information pack. Alternatively visit our website at www.youngwriters.co.uk

Write to:
Young Writers Information,
Remus House,
Coltsfoot Drive,
Peterborough,
PE2 9JX

Tel: (01733) 890066
Email: youngwriters@forwardpress.co.uk